Making a Meal for a DRAGON

by Ruth Owen

BEARPORT PUBLISHING

Minneapolis, Minnesota

Credits:
Cover, © Shutterstock and © Ruth Owen Books; 1, © shaineast/Shutterstock and © Ruth Owen Books; 3, © Shutterstock; 4T, © Studio 77 FX/Shutterstock; 4, © Ruth Owen Books; 5, © Shutterstock; 6T, © Studio 77 FX/Shutterstock; 6B, © Shutterstock and © Ruth Owen Books; 7, © Ruth Owen Books; 8–9, © Ruth Owen Books and © Shutterstock; 10T, © patrimonio designs ltd/Shutterstock; 10B, © Ruth Owen Books; 11, © Ruth Owen Books; 12–13, © Ruth Owen Books and © Shutterstock; 14T, © shaineast/Shutterstock; 14B, © Ruth Owen Books; 15, © Ruth Owen Books; 16–17, © Ruth Owen Books; 18T, © Pariyah Pariyah/Shutterstock; 18B, © Ruth Owen Books; 19, © Ruth Owen Books; 20–21, © Ruth Owen Books; 22T, © tsuneomp/Shutterstock; 22C, © eddystocker/Shutterstock; 22B, © Lefteris Papaulakis/Shutterstock; 23TL, © Lazy Bear/Shutterstock; 23TR, © Pixel-shot/Shutterstock; 23BR, © Raimond Klavins/Shutterstock.

President: Jen Jenson
Director of Product Development: Spencer Brinker
Senior Editor: Allison Juda
Associate Editor: Charly Haley
Designer: Colin O'Dea

Library of Congress Cataloging-in-Publication Data

Names: Owen, Ruth, 1967- author.
Title: Making a meal for a dragon / by Ruth Owen.
Description: Create! books. | Minneapolis, Minnesota : Bearport Publishing Company, [2022] | Series: Mythical meals | Includes bibliographical references and index.
Identifiers: LCCN 2021003347 (print) | LCCN 2021003348 (ebook) | ISBN 9781636910703 (library binding) | ISBN 9781636910772 (ebook)
Subjects: LCSH: Cooking—Juvenile literature. | LCGFT: Cookbooks.
Classification: LCC TX652.5 .O962 2022 (print) | LCC TX652.5 (ebook) | DDC 641.5—dc23
LC record available at https://lccn.loc.gov/2021003347
LC ebook record available at https://lccn.loc.gov/2021003348

Copyright © 2022 Bearport Publishing Company. All rights reserved. No part of this publication may be reproduced in whole or in part, stored in any retrieval system, or transmitted in any form or by any means, electronic, mechanical, photocopying, recording, or otherwise, without written permission from the publisher.

For more information, write to Bearport Publishing, 5357 Penn Avenue South, Minneapolis, MN 55419. Printed in the United States of America.

Contents

A Feast for a Dragon 4

Drink
Fiery Ginger Fizz 6

Appetizer
Crunchy Claws and Dip 10

Main Course
Dragon Pie 14

Dessert
Dragon's Breath Kisses 18

Fire-Breathing Dragons 22
Glossary 23
Index 24
Read More 24
Learn More Online 24
About the Author 24

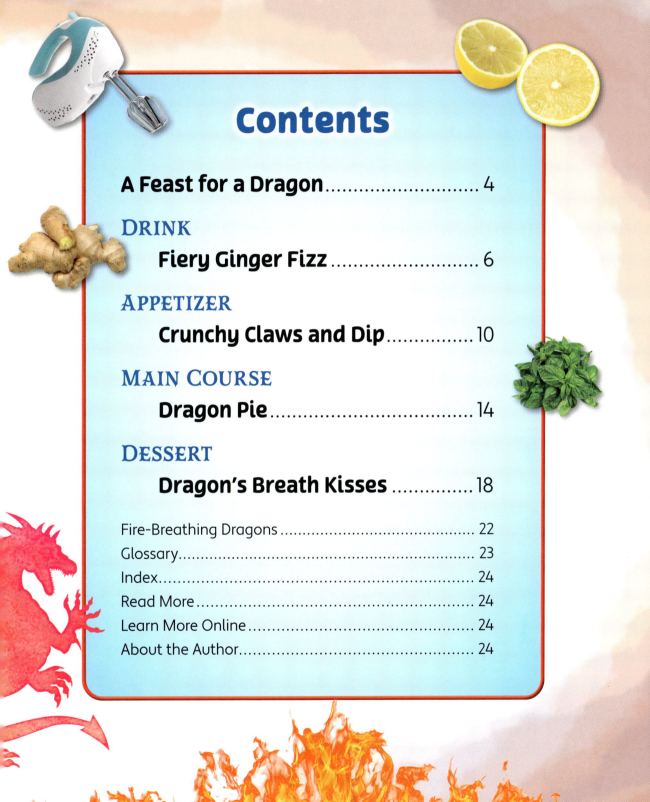

A Feast for a Dragon

With a flap of her giant wings, your dragon dinner guest has arrived! Get ready to make your new friend a **feast** that will satisfy her big **appetite**.

◀ **Drink**
Give your dragon a huge welcome by serving her this sweet and spicy ginger drink.

Appetizer ▶
Celebrate your dinner guest's claws by making these crunchy, claw-shaped **turmeric** crackers.

◀ **Main Course**
Your **carnivorous** friend will love this pepperoni pie that's shaped and colored like a dragon.

Dessert ▶
Finish the meal for the fire-breather with some sweet, flame-colored meringue kisses!

4

Get Ready to Cook!

- Always wash your hands with soap and hot water before you start cooking.
- Make sure your work surface and your cooking **equipment** are clean.
- Carefully read the recipe before you begin. If there's a step you don't understand, ask an adult for help.
- Gather all your supplies before you start.
- Carefully measure your **ingredients**. Your cooking will go better if you use the right amounts.
- When you've finished cooking, clean up the kitchen. Wash, dry, and put away your equipment.

Be Safe!

For some recipes, you'll need an adult helper. Be sure to ask for help when you use:

- Sharp objects, such as knives or scissors
- The oven, stove, or microwave
- An electric hand mixer

DRINK
Fiery Ginger Fizz

Your dragon friend can blast flames from her mouth and puff smoke from her nostrils. So, she needs a drink with a big, strong flavor. This homemade ginger drink will hit the spot!

Makes 4 servings

Ingredients

- 5 oz (140 g) fresh ginger root, washed
- 4 tablespoons dark brown sugar
- 3 lemons, washed
- 4 cups plain seltzer water
- 2 cups ice cubes
- 4 stems fresh mint, washed

Equipment

- A knife
- A grater
- A mixing bowl
- Clean scissors
- A pestle, a rolling pin, or another heavy object for crushing
- A lemon juicer
- A small bowl
- A wooden spoon
- A spoon for tasting
- A strainer
- A pitcher
- 4 glasses

Ginger root →

1 Ginger root grows in very strange shapes! Ask an adult helper to cut the ginger into pieces that are easy to grate.

Grater →

← Grated ginger

2 Very carefully grate the ginger into a mixing bowl. It's fine to include any skin and juice. To protect your fingers from the grater, be sure to stop grating once you have about an inch (2.5 cm) left. Ask your helper to grate these smaller pieces.

3 Add the brown sugar to the bowl.

← Brown sugar

4 Ask your helper to peel the rind from two lemons. Then, use scissors to cut the rind into small pieces and add them to the bowl.

Rind ↓

5 Now, crush the ingredients to mix the flavors. You can use a pestle, the end of a rolling pin, or another heavy object.

Pestle

Mortar

A pestle and mortar are used for crushing ingredients in cooking.

6 Ask your adult helper to cut all three lemons in half. With a lemon juicer, juice the lemons. Add the juice to a small bowl and remove any seeds. Pour the juice into the bowl with the ginger, sugar, and lemon rind.

7 Add the seltzer to the bowl. Stir the mixture with a wooden spoon and then allow it to sit for 10 minutes to let the flavors **infuse**.

8 Use a spoon to taste the drink. If it's too sour, add a little bit more sugar.

Pour the mixture here.

Strainer

Pitcher

Leftover mixture

9 Ask your helper to hold a strainer over the top of a pitcher. Then, carefully pour the ginger mixture through the strainer into the pitcher. The strainer will catch the pieces of ginger root and lemon rind.

10 Add some ice cubes to each of the four glasses.

11 Pour the ginger fizz into the glasses, dividing it equally.

12 Finally, add a stem of mint to each glass for decoration and serve immediately.

A DELICIOUS DRAGONY DRINK!

★ ★ ★ ★ ★ APPETIZER ★ ★ ★ ★ ★
Crunchy Claws and Dip

Your dinner guest hunts by swooping from the sky to grab a cow, sheep, or goat in her powerful **talons**. Start your feast by grabbing delicious dip with these crunchy, claw-shaped crackers.

Makes 6 servings

Ingredients

- 1 ⅓ cups plus 1 tablespoon all-purpose flour
- ½ teaspoon baking powder
- 1 ½ teaspoons salt
- 1 ½ teaspoons turmeric
- 1 teaspoon cumin
- 1 teaspoon plus 1 tablespoon olive oil
- ½ cup water
- 1 cup sliced roasted red peppers
- 1 can cannellini beans (also called white kidney beans)
- ¼ cup fresh basil leaves, stems removed
- 3 tablespoons shredded Parmesan cheese
- 2 cloves garlic, peeled
- ½ teaspoon black pepper
- 1 lemon

Equipment

- A large baking sheet
- Parchment paper
- A mixing bowl
- A metal spoon
- A rolling pin
- A 4-inch (10 cm) round cookie cutter
- A blender
- A teaspoon
- A small bowl
- A large platter

1. Ask an adult helper to preheat the oven to 400°F (200°C). Line a baking sheet with parchment paper.

2. Add 1 ⅓ cups of flour, the baking powder, ½ teaspoon of salt, the turmeric powder, the cumin powder, 1 teaspoon of olive oil, and the water to a mixing bowl. Stir the ingredients with a metal spoon. Then, mix and squeeze the mixture with your hands to form a ball of **dough**.

3. **Dust** your work surface with a tablespoon of flour. Use a rolling pin to roll out the dough until it is thinner than this book's cover.

4. Use the cookie cutter to cut a circle of dough. Move the circle away from the rest of the dough.

5 Next, position the cookie cutter near the edge of the circle so that you create a claw-shaped section and cut. Then, cut a second claw from the other side of the circle. Put both claws on the baking pan. Set aside any dough scraps.

6 Repeat steps 4 and 5 until you can't cut any more circles. Then, squeeze the leftover scraps of dough together and roll them out again. Continue to cut circles and claws until you've used up all the dough.

7 Ask your adult helper to put the claw crackers into the oven and bake them for 15 minutes.

Basil

Garlic cloves

Roasted red peppers

Cannellini beans

Grated Parmesan

8 To make the dip, put the basil, garlic, peppers, beans, and Parmesan cheese into a blender.

9 Add 1 tablespoon of olive oil, 1 teaspoon of salt, and ½ teaspoon of ground black pepper to the blender.

10 Ask your helper to cut the lemon in half. Take one half and remove any seeds with a teaspoon. Then, squeeze all the juice from that lemon half into the blender.

11 Blend the dip ingredients together for about 30 seconds. The mixture should be smooth.

Blended dip

12 When the crackers are done, allow them to cool on the baking sheet for about 15 minutes. Spoon the dip into a small bowl and place it in the center of a large platter. Arrange the cooled crackers around the bowl of dip and serve.

A CLAW-SOME START TO YOUR MEAL!

MAIN COURSE
Dragon Pie

Sometimes your friend may cook her **prey** with a blast of her fiery breath! She won't be able to wait to take a bite of this steaming-hot pie, packed with pepperoni.

Makes 6 servings

Ingredients

- 4 ½ cups all-purpose flour
- 2 sticks cold butter, cut into cubes
- 1 teaspoon salt
- 2 eggs
- Water
- Orange and green food coloring
- 2 cups pepperoni slices
- 2 large tomatoes, thinly sliced
- 2 cups shredded cheddar or mozzarella cheese
- 1 cup tomato sauce
- 1 tablespoon Italian seasoning

Equipment

- A mixing bowl
- Measuring cups
- 2 small bowls
- Parchment paper
- Measuring spoons
- A rolling pin
- A butter knife
- A whisk
- A large baking sheet
- A fork
- A pastry brush
- A teaspoon

1 Put 4 cups of flour, the butter, and salt into a mixing bowl. With your fingers, rub the butter into the flour and salt until the mixture looks like breadcrumbs. Set aside 1 ½ cups of the mixture in a small bowl.

2 Break an egg into the mixing bowl and add 5 tablespoons of water. Then, gently mix and squeeze with your hands until the ingredients form a ball of soft dough. Wrap the dough in parchment paper and put it in the refrigerator to chill for 30 minutes.

Ball of dough

Parchment paper

orange dough

3 Add a tablespoon of water and 10 drops of orange food coloring to the small bowl containing the flour, salt, and butter mixture. Mix and squeeze it with your hands to form a small ball of orange dough.

Horns

Triangular spikes

The dragon horns in this picture are 3 in. (7.5 cm) long, but you can make yours any size or shape you'd like.

4 Dust your work surface with a little of the remaining flour. Use a rolling pin to roll out the orange dough until it's about ¼ in. (0.6 cm) thick. With the tip of a butter knife, draw some dragon horns onto the dough and then carefully cut them out. Shape the remaining orange dough into 8 triangular spikes.

Rectangle of dough

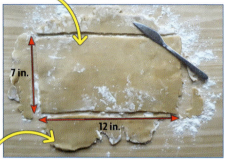
Extra dough

5. Break an egg into the second small bowl. Add 5 drops of green food coloring and whisk together. Put to one side.

6. Ask an adult helper to preheat the oven to 325°F (163°C). Then, take the dough from the fridge and divide it in half. Dust your work surface again. Use a rolling pin to roll each half into a rectangle slightly bigger than 12 x 7 in. (30.4 x 18 cm) and the thickness of this book's cover. Use a butter knife to trim all the sides of both rectangles. Set aside the extra dough.

Tuck

7. Place one dough rectangle on a baking sheet. Make a little tuck in one of the long sides so that the rectangle is slightly curved.

8. Arrange a layer of pepperoni slices on the piece of dough. Leave about ¾ in. (1.9 cm) uncovered around all four edges. Next, add a layer of tomato slices on top of the pepperoni. Then, add some tomato sauce, shredded cheese, and Italian seasoning. Repeat the layers of filling until all the ingredients are used up.

9 Take the second dough rectangle and lay it over the pie filling. Use a fork to press the edges of the two rectangles together. Then, shape each end of the pie to make it narrower than the center.

10 Squeeze the extra dough into a ball and use the rolling pin to roll it out. Use a butter knife to cut a triangle for the dragon's head and a forked tail. Roll some dough into two small balls for the dragon's eyes. Brush some of the green egg mixture onto the pie and use it like glue to stick on the head, eyes, and tail.

Tip of teaspoon

11 Use the tip of a teaspoon to gently make small curves in rows that look like **scales**. Then, use the brush to paint the dragon with the green egg mixture. Press on the orange horns and spikes. Finally, use the butter knife to add grooves to the dragon's eyes.

12 Ask your helper to put the pie into the bottom half of the oven and bake it for 55 minutes. When it's done, enjoy!

A BIG TREAT FOR A BIG EATER

17

DESSERT
Dragon's Breath Kisses

Your guest could probably bake these treats in a second with one fiery breath. But they might end up a little black and burned. So, let's stick to using an oven to bake these flame-like meringues to finish off your meal.

Makes 7 servings

Ingredients

- 3 large egg whites
- A pinch of salt
- ½ cup granulated sugar
- 1 teaspoon vanilla extract
- Orange and red food coloring
- ¾ cup powdered sugar

Equipment

- A baking sheet
- Parchment paper
- A mixing bowl
- An electric hand mixer
- A teaspoon
- A wooden spoon
- A piping bag fitted with a wide nozzle
- A glass
- A thin, clean paintbrush

1. Ask an adult helper to preheat the oven to 200°F (93°C). Line a baking sheet with parchment paper.

2. Put the egg whites and salt into a mixing bowl. **Beat** the egg whites with an electric hand mixer until they look smooth, thick, and white.

3. Next, add a spoonful of granulated sugar and beat for about 45 seconds with the mixer. Repeat until all the granulated sugar has been added and the mixture looks thick and shiny.

> To test if the meringue is ready, turn off the mixer. Then, use the beaters to gently lift small amounts of the meringue. If you can make the meringue stand up in stiff little mountain peaks, it is ready.

4. Finally, add the vanilla extract, ¼ teaspoon of orange food coloring, and the powdered sugar to the mixing bowl. Then, use a spoon to gently **fold** them into the meringue mixture.

5 Place the tip end of the piping bag into a glass. Then, roll the top of the bag down over the sides of the glass so that you can easily reach the inside of the piping bag.

6 Next, use your brush to paint stripes of red food coloring on the inside of the bag. Make sure that the stripes go all the way down to the tip.

7 Spoon the orange meringue mixture into the piping bag. As the bag fills up, gradually unroll it from the glass. Leave about 2 in. (5 cm) unfilled at the top for you to hold.

8 Slowly and carefully squeeze some meringue onto the baking sheet. Make a flame about 1 ½ in. (3.8 cm) high.

9 Then, pipe a second meringue flame shape next to the first so that they are touching. Pipe a third flame that touches the other two. Your first dragon's breath kiss is ready.

10 Repeat steps 8 and 9 until the piping bag is empty. If you still have some meringue left in the mixing bowl, wash and dry the piping bag. Then, repeat steps 5 through 9 until all the meringue is used up.

11 Ask your helper to put the baking sheet onto the center rack of the oven.

12 Bake the meringues for 2 ½ hours. Then, turn off the oven and leave the baking sheet inside until the oven is completely cool. This will help the meringues harden and keep them from cracking.

SWEET KISSES FOR A FIERCE DRAGON!

Fire-Breathing Dragons

Get to know more about your dinner guest by reading these fascinating **myths** about dragons.

In old stories, some dragons are described as small and others are super large! They are said to live in the sea or in mountain caves.

What dragon eggs might look like

Dragons are thought to hatch from eggs. The mother dragon brings them food. But even baby dragons are fierce—they can look after themselves.

The fossil of a Megaraptor dinosaur

Dragon stories have been told around the world for thousands of years. But how did these tales get started? It's possible that when people long ago found **fossilized** dinosaur bones, they thought the bones belonged to dragons.

IF YOU WERE HAVING DINNER WITH A DRAGON, WHAT WOULD YOU LIKE TO ASK HER?

Glossary

appetite a desire for food and drink

beat to mix ingredients until they are smooth using a spoon, fork, whisk, or electric mixer

carnivorous meat-eating

dough a mixture of flour, water, and other ingredients that is used to make crusts, bread, or cookies

dust to sprinkle with flour to keep dough from sticking

equipment tools or items that are used to do a job

feast a large meal with lots of different dishes

fold to mix in an ingredient by lifting the mixture as you very gently stir it

fossilized turned to rock over millions of years

infuse to soak into a liquid

ingredients the things that are used to make food

myths old stories that tell of strange or magical events and creatures

prey an animal that is hunted by other animals for food

scales small, overlapping, plate-like coverings on an animal's body

talons sharp claws

turmeric a spice made from the root of the turmeric plant

23

Index

baby dragons 22
claws 4, 10, 12–13
dinosaurs 22
dragon eggs 22
fire 4, 22
hunting 10
mother dragons 22
myths 22
safety 5

Read More

Doeden, Matt. *Dragons (Mythical Creatures)*. North Mankato, MN: Picture Window Books, 2020.

Gish, Ashley. *Dragons (Amazing Mysteries)*. Mankato, MN: Creative Education, 2020.

Learn More Online

1. Go to **www.factsurfer.com**
2. Enter **"Dragon Meals"** into the search box.
3. Click on the cover of this book to see a list of websites.

About the Author

Ruth Owen has been developing and writing children's books for more than 10 years. She lives in Cornwall, England, just minutes from the ocean. Ruth loves cooking and making up recipes. Her favorite dish in this book is the dragon pie because it's great fun to make and decorate the dragon!